In the Van

by Diana Noonan
illustrated by Julie Knoblock

 Harcourt
SCHOOL PUBLISHERS

Printed in the United States of America

ISBN 10: 0-15-350605-9
ISBN 13: 978-0-15-350605-5

Ordering Options
ISBN 10: 0-15-350598-2 (Grade 1 On-Level Collection)
ISBN 13: 978-0-15-350598-0 (Grade 1 On-Level Collection)
ISBN 10: 0-15-357747-9 (package of 5)
ISBN 13: 978-0-15-357747-5 (package of 5)

2 3 4 5 6 7 8 9 10   179   15 14 13 12 11 10 09 08 07

Look in the van.

I like this bag.

No. I like that bag.

I like this hat.

No. I like that hat.

I like this little cat.

I like this little cat, too.